WHY THE SNAKE CRAWLS ON ITS BELLY

by Eric Kimmel
Illustrated by Allen Davis

THE LIBRARY
TEMPLE JUDEA MIZPAH
SKOKIE, ILLINOIS

PITSPOPANY

NEW YORK ◆ JERUSALEM

Published by Pitspopany Press
Text Copyright © 2001 by Eric A. Kimmel
Illustrations Copyright © 2001 by Allen Davis

Cover Design: Benjie Herskowitz

All rights reserved. No part of this book may be reproduced or
transmitted in any form or by any means, electronic or mechanical,
including photocopying, recording, or by any information storage and
retrieval system, without permission in writing from the publisher.

Cloth ISBN: 1-930143-20-6

Pitspopany Press titles may be purchased for fundraising programs
by schools and organizations by contacting:

Marketing Director, Pitspopany Press
40 East 78th Street, Suite 16D
New York, New York 10021
Tel: (800) 232-2931
Fax: (212) 472-6253
Email: pop@netvision.net.il
Web Site: www.pitspopany com

Printed in Israel

To Yaacov,
Who loves the story

Eric

To Carol,
My wonderful Eve in our Garden

Allen

ANIMAL STORIES FOR CHILDREN
From PITSPOPANY PRESS

Seven Animal Stories For Children
by Howard & Mary K. Bogot

Seven Animals Wag Their Tales
by Howard & Mary K. Bogot

The Littlest Frog
by Sylvia Rouss

The Littlest Pair
by Sylvia Rouss

The Littlest Candlesticks
by Sylvia Rouss

The Rooster Prince
(Storytelling World Award Winner)
by Sydell Waxman

WHY DID THE SNAKE LOSE ITS LEGS?

WHEN ADAM AND EVE were in the Garden of Eden they traveled freely between Earth and Heaven, just as a person who lives in his house moves freely up and down, from the ground floor to the attic.

AFTER THE SNAKE convinced Eve to eat from the Tree of Knowledge, Adam and Eve were no longer allowed to climb up to their attic, to climb up to Heaven.

FOR CUTTING OFF Adam and Eve from freely moving between Earth and Heaven, the snake lost its legs.

Ohr Ha'Chaim, Commentary on Genesis 3:14

THE LIBRARY
TEMPLE JUDEA MIZPAH
SKOKIE, ILLINOIS

In the beginning God created the world and all the creatures in it. He created the man and the woman in His image.

He called the man Adam and the woman Eve.

Because God created Adam and Eve in His own image, He had a special love for them that set them apart from all other creatures. Adam and Eve talked with God every day. God was their father, and they were His children.

IN THOSE DAYS, A LADDER STOOD BETWEEN HEAVEN AND EARTH.
ADAM AND EVE COULD CLIMB THAT LADDER ALL THE WAY TO HEAVEN.
THEY FLEW ABOVE THE CLOUDS WITH THE SERAPHIM.
THEY SANG HYMNS OF PRAISE WITH THE OPHANIM.
THEY STUDIED TORAH WITH THE HEAVENLY BEINGS.

THEY EVEN CLIMBED UP TO GOD'S THRONE, AND
RESTED IN THE BOSOM OF THE ONE WHO CREATED THEM.

GOD REVEALED THE WONDERS OF CREATION TO EVE AND ADAM. HE SHOWED THEM THE GREAT FISH LEVIATHAN, WHO LIVES AT THE BOTTOM OF THE OCEAN.

THEY BEHELD THE MIGHTY **ZIZ**, THE KING OF BIRDS, WHO BUILDS HER NEST ON THE TALLEST PEAKS.

All of God's creatures loved Adam and Eve – except Nakhash, the snake. Nakhash was the cleverest, most beautiful of all the animals. He alone could walk on his hind legs like a human being. Like human beings, he also possessed the power of speech.

Nakhash would have been lord of the animals, had God not created Adam and Eve. Nakhash thought to himself, "If I can trick Adam and Eve into disobeying God, God will turn against them. Then I will take back my rightful place."

So Nakhash set a trap for Adam and Eve. He caused them to eat the fruit of the Tree of Knowledge, which God had forbidden.

EVERY TIME NAKHASH SPOKE A FALSE WORD, AND
EVERY TIME ADAM AND EVE LISTENED, A RUNG ON
THE LADDER BETWEEN HEAVEN AND EARTH
SHATTERED. THE BROKEN PIECES FELL TO EARTH AS
SHOOTING STARS. THEY BECAME DIAMONDS, RUBIES,
AND OTHER PRECIOUS STONES; TINY FRAGMENTS OF
THE RICHES OF HEAVEN.

When God discovered what Adam and Eve had done, He became very sad. Adam and Eve could no longer stay in the beautiful garden He created for them. They had to go out into the world and toil for the food they ate. They would know sorrow and pain, and at the end of their lives, death. They could no longer climb the ladder to Heaven, for all its rungs had been broken. No longer would human beings be able to visit the heights of Heaven or sing with the angels.

WITH A HEAVY HEART, GOD DECREED ADAM AND EVE'S PUNISHMENT. THEN HE SAID TO THE ANGELS, "WHAT SHALL BE DONE WITH NAKHASH, THE SNAKE? ADAM AND EVE WOULD NEVER HAVE DISOBEYED ME HAD IT NOT BEEN FOR NAKHASH'S LYING WORDS."

THE ANGEL GABRIEL SPOKE FIRST. "TAKE AWAY HIS EYES. NAKHASH SAW THE LOVE YOU HAD FOR ADAM AND EVE. HIS EYES CAUSED HIM TO DO EVIL, SO LET HIS EYES BE TAKEN AWAY. LET HIM BE BLIND."

THE ANGEL RAFAEL SPOKE NEXT. "NAKHASH USED HIS MOUTH TO SPEAK FALSE WORDS INTO THE HEARTS OF ADAM AND EVE. TAKE AWAY HIS MOUTH. LET HIM LOSE THE POWER TO SPEAK."

NOW THE ANGEL MICHAEL SPOKE. "NAKHASH'S ARMS REACHED OUT TO GRASP WHAT ADAM AND EVE POSSESSED. GREED LED HIM TO DO WRONG, SO TAKE AWAY HIS ARMS. LET HIM NEVER REACH OUT TO EVIL AGAIN."

FINALLY, THE ANGEL AZRIEL SPOKE. "NAKHASH CAUSED ADAM AND EVE TO BE
DRIVEN OUT OF THE GARDEN. HIS FALSE WORDS DESTROYED THE LADDER TO
HEAVEN. ONCE ADAM AND EVE COULD CLIMB THAT LADDER TO BE WITH THE AN-
GELS. NOW THEIR FACES ARE LOWERED IN SHAME. LOWER NAKHASH'S FACE, TOO.
TAKE AWAY HIS LEGS, SO HE CANNOT STAND UP TO LOOK UP AT THE SKY. LET HIM
CRAWL ON HIS BELLY."

God spoke to the snake. "Nakhash, the angels have spoken. All these punishments are just. What do you have to say?"

Nakhash lowered his eyes as he confessed his guilt. "Jealousy and anger led me to do wrong. I am sorry. My wickedness brought suffering into the world. My misdeeds broke the ladder to heaven. I cannot ask for mercy. I deserve the harshest punishment. Let me die."

But God did not agree. "Death is what you deserve. However, because you accepted your guilt and did not try to blame

OTHERS, I WILL SHOW MERCY. YOU WILL NOT DIE. HOWEVER, YOU WILL NO LONGER BE THE CREATURE YOU ARE. YOU MUST BE CHANGED, SO YOU CAN NEVER DECEIVE ANYONE AGAIN. YOU MAY KEEP YOUR EYES, BUT I WILL TAKE YOUR EYELIDS. BECAUSE YOU LOOKED AT EVIL WITHOUT BLINKING, YOUR EYES WILL NEVER BLINK AGAIN. THEY WILL REMAIN OPEN, WHEN YOU WAKE AND WHEN YOU SLEEP.

"BECAUSE YOUR MOUTH AND TONGUE DID WRONG, I WILL TAKE AWAY YOUR LIPS. NEVER AGAIN WILL YOU HAVE THE POWER OF SPEECH. I WILL SPLIT YOUR TONGUE IN TWO, AS A SIGN THAT YOU TOLD LIES. THE TONGUE THAT DECEIVED ADAM AND EVE WILL LICK THE DUST OF THE EARTH.

"THE LEGS THAT RAN TO DO EVIL AND THE ARMS THAT REACHED OUT TO HARM OTHERS WILL ALSO BE TAKEN AWAY.

But I will give you something in return. When your skin becomes old and worn, it will split. You will crawl out, a new creature in a shining skin. No matter how old you become, you will always appear to be young and beautiful.

"This will be a sign to Adam and Eve, and all their descendants. Whenever they see a snake shedding its skin, they will understand that they have the power to change themselves. Like the snake, they can cast off all that is selfish and wicked in their daily lives. They can shed their old ways like a snake's worn-out skin and become new again."

So it has been since the days when the world was new. Snakes crawl on their bellies. Their tongues lick the dirt. Their eyes remain open, awake and asleep. And when they grow drab and worn, they shed their skins and renew themselves.

So it will be until the END OF DAYS, when GOD WILL RESTORE THE LADDER BETWEEN HEAVEN AND EARTH. THE CHILDREN OF ADAM AND EVE WILL ONCE AGAIN CLIMB UP TO HEAVEN AND WALK WITH THE ANGELS.

AND THE CHILDREN OF NAKHASH, THE SNAKE, WILL WALK BESIDE THEM.

THE LIBRARY
TEMPLE JUDEA
SKOKIE, ILLINOIS